Duck and Rooster

Written by Jill Eggleton
Illustrated by Kelvin Hawley

Rooster went on the fence.

Duck went on the grass.

"Come up here," said Rooster.

"Come on the fence."

Duck went on the fence.
Rooster went on the roof.

"Come up here," said Rooster.

Duck went on the roof.
Rooster went on
the chimney.

"Come up here,"
said Rooster.

Duck went on
the chimney, too.

Oops!

"Look at Rooster," said Duck.

"Rooster is in the chimney!"

"Come up here," said Duck.

A Flow Diagram

Guide Notes

Title: Duck and Rooster
Stage: Early (1) – Red

Genre: Fiction
Approach: Guided Reading
Processes: Thinking Critically, Exploring Language, Processing Information
Written and Visual Focus: Flow Diagram, Speech Bubble
Word Count: 71

THINKING CRITICALLY
(sample questions)
- What do you think this story could be about?
- Look at the title and read it to the children.
- Why do you think Rooster wanted Duck to copy him?
- Why do you think Rooster fell down the chimney?
- How do you think Rooster will get out of the chimney?
- Where do you think it would be safe and sensible for Duck and Rooster to be?

EXPLORING LANGUAGE

Terminology
Title, cover, illustrations, author, illustrator

Vocabulary
Interest words: fence, grass, chimney, roof, oops
High-frequency words: up, too
Positional words: on, up, in

Print Conventions
Capital letter for sentence beginnings and names (**R**ooster, **D**uck), periods, commas, quotation marks, exclamation mark